Men at Work

Mike Gayle

WITHDRAWN FROM STOCK

HODDER

First published in Great Britain in 2010 by Hodder & Stoughton
An Hachette UK company

1

Copyright © Mike Gayle 2010

The right of Mike Gayle to be identified as the Author of the
Work has been asserted by him in accordance with the
Copyright, Designs and Patents Act 1988.

All rights reserved. No part of this publication may be
reproduced, stored in a retrieval system, or transmitted, in any
form or by any means without the prior written permission of
the publisher, nor be otherwise circulated in any form of
binding or cover other than that in which it is published and
without a similar condition being imposed on the subsequent
purchaser.

All characters in this publication are fictitious and any
resemblance to real persons, living or dead, is purely coincidental.

A CIP catalogue record for this title is available from the
British Library

ISBN 978 1 444 71177 6

Typeset in Stone Serif by Palimpsest Book Production Limited,
Falkirk, Stirlingshire

Hodd   atural,
renewal   l grown
in susta   rocesses
are ex   ons of

LIBRARIES NI	
C700544498	
RONDO	08/02/2011
F	£ 1.99
NEHQP	

www.hodder.co.uk

Chapter 1

"What would you do if you won the Lottery?"

It was just after ten on a Sunday night in May and thirty-one-year-old Ian Greening was sitting in the Red Lion with his girlfriend Emma Kavanagh having one of their amusing but daft conversations.

"How much are we talking?" asked Ian. "Many millions or just the one?"

Emma considered the question. "Many," she said after a few moments. "I reckon you'd need six or seven million to totally change your life."

"Cool," said Ian. "Six or seven, eh? Where to begin? Well, it's obvious that I'd buy us a new house with his 'n' her bathrooms so that I wouldn't have to walk over your underwear to get to the shower. Then maybe I'd pay off my mum and dad's mortgage. A luxury yacht would be nice and I'd get myself a season ticket for the Blues. Actually scrub that. I'm a millionaire now, aren't I? So I'd be able to afford a box at the Blues!" He glanced over at Emma and grinned. "Oh, and I suppose I'd have to take you on the

1

holiday of a lifetime because if I didn't you'd moan at me for the rest of my life."

"And is that it?" asked Emma.

"Obviously I'd buy a few flash cars. You know the drill, a couple of Ferraris and maybe a Range Rover for when I need to take you to Tesco's but other than that I think I'm pretty much done."

"And what about work?"

"What about work?"

"Well, I assume we'd both give up work. So what would you do with all your spare time, you know, when we weren't jetting about or lounging on our yacht?"

Ian laughed. "What are you talking about? I'd be more than happy for you to give up work, but what makes you think I would?"

Emma stared at him in amazement. "So you're telling me that if you won seven million pounds on the Lottery you would still get up every morning, make your way through the traffic to get to work, put in your eight hours and then fight your way home again, even though you didn't have to?"

"Yeah, of course I would," replied Ian. "There's no way I'd ever give up work. Not in a million years. Not even for seven million pounds."

"But why not?" said Emma, more than a little bit confused by her boyfriend's reply. "Why would you carry on working in what – no offence, babe – is a temp job that you never quite found the energy to leave?"

"I just would," said Ian.

"Why?"

"I just would. There's no reason. I just would."

"BUT WHY?"

There was a silence and then Ian said, "Because I love my job, okay?"

Emma looked at him. Her face was puzzled. "I know you like your job but *you* actually *love it*?"

Ian nodded. "It's true! I don't care who knows it. I love my job."

"Yeah, but when you say you love it, you really mean that you like it a lot, don't you?"

Ian shook his head. "Nope, when I say I love it, I really do mean that I love it. I adore it. If my job could get up and move around I would follow it and kiss the ground it walked on. That's how much I love my job."

"But you don't love it more than anything else in your life do you? For instance, you don't love it more than those awful sandwiches you're always making?"

"You mean the Greening Cheese Wonder?" Ian felt hungry at the very thought. "Ham, cheese, Branston pickle, with a layer of crushed salt and vinegar crisps all wedged between two slices of white bread and garnished with a half radish?" Emma nodded as Ian found himself wiping a line of drool from the corner of his mouth. "Yeah of course I love work more than those."

"Okay," said Emma, clearly still wanting to make her point. "How about your comic collection? I can't believe for a minute that you love work more than those X-Factor things you're always going on about."

Ian sighed heavily. "X-Men, Emma. They're called X-Men."

"X-Men, X-People what's the difference?"

"What's the difference?" Ian couldn't believe what he was hearing. Only last week he had sat Emma down to explain why Wolverine and Sabretooth were sworn enemies. "I'll tell you what the difference is, young lady! One is a group of cool outlaw mutants who are forever saving the universe from certain doom and the other isn't!"

"Fine!" said Emma crossly. "X-Men it is! But the question is, do you love your job more than your X-Men comics?"

"Yes!" snapped Ian. He was getting cross with Emma for getting cross with him. "I do indeed love my job more than I love my X-Men comics, okay?"

"No," said Emma. "Not okay. I'm still finding it hard to believe that you love your job more than those dusty old comics because you won't let me anywhere near them! But that's fine. I don't mind. Let's take a look at this. You love your job more than you love those stupid sandwiches and more than your comic collection. My final question to you is this . . . do you love your job more than me?"

Ian looked at Emma and could see that she was deadly serious. Emma, his girlfriend of the last six years, really wanted an answer and she wasn't going to take any old rubbish. "Oh, Em!" he said with a sigh. "If you have to ask, then all I can say is that you really don't know me at all."

Chapter 2

One year later

"Moonwalk! Moonwalk! Moonwalk!"

It was just after ten on a Friday night in May and a very, very drunk Ian Greening was being hounded by his chanting workmates. They wanted him to climb onto the table and perform the "It looks like I'm going forwards but actually I'm going backwards" dance routine made world famous by Michael Jackson. And the reason they wanted Ian to do his Michael Jackson dance routine was simple – they wanted a laugh. Ian worked on the fourth floor of Holling House in the Policy Planning department of the Department of Work and Pensions in Birmingham. And as far as the workers there were concerned, Ian Greening *was* a laugh and had been ever since his first day at work eight years ago.

Although Ian had usually worked in poorly paid jobs, he had always managed to make them fun. For instance, when Ian had worked at a large

DIY store he had organised trolley races along the aisles whenever the store was quiet. When he worked at a petrol station near Ladywood he had made up a game called the "Carless Car Wash Challenge". This involved trying to find out which member of staff could stand in the car wash in borrowed Scuba gear the longest.

Then there was the time that he worked as an orderly at Selly Oak Hospital. He got the other orderlies to join him during their break in a game of 101 Uses for a Non-Latex Glove. Whatever the job and whatever the situation, Ian had never doubted that there was a way of making it fun. But that was then.

Ian had been just twenty-three when he joined the fourth floor of the Department of Work and Pensions as a temp in what was then known as the "Office of No Hope". On his first morning, he walked up to the drab concrete building and watched his fellow workers, armed with their passes, make their way through security up to the fourth floor. And he had wondered whether he was about to make the mistake of his life. He had never seen a building quite so grey or fellow workers who looked quite so beaten down by the daily grind of the work routine. This would either be his worst defeat or his greatest success.

Five hours later, as he moonwalked across a

row of tables in the local pub, having talked half the office into coming for a lunchtime drink, he found out. The people who staffed the "Office of No Hope" were nowhere near as boring as he had feared they might be. In fact they were the best bunch of people he had ever had the pleasure of working with. All they needed to bring out their inner party demon was a bit of booze, a smattering of Eighties music and a bit of moonwalking. Even after eight years of performances at their after work drinks dos, that always got a laugh.

Sometime later on that Friday night in May, he had led the entire room through several different karaoke versions of Queen's greatest hits. And done an impression of his line manager that was so accurate that even people who didn't know him were crying with laughter. Then Ian decided to make his way home.

A little bit worse for wear, he looked around for a taxi and was relieved when, after ten minutes, one pulled up next to him. He jumped into the back, settled into his seat and mumbled his address to the driver. He pulled out his phone to check his messages. Just as he had expected, there were well over a dozen texts from his work mates thanking him for making Big Friday (as he had christened it) such a laugh and saying it was the highlight of their week. Ian always felt good when he read these messages. As though he had found his place in the world. It made him feel as if simply by turning up to work and being himself he was doing a good thing.

He saw that he had a few missed calls from his girlfriend, Emma. He thought about checking his voicemail but then he got sidetracked recalling just how funny his impression of his line manager had been. He then fell asleep, only waking up as the cab pulled up outside their two-bedroom terrace in Bearwood.

Ian handed the cabbie a ten pound note, told him to keep the change and made his way into his house. He headed straight for the kitchen to grab a glass of water in the hope of staving off the hangover he knew would be coming his way.

With his glass in hand, he was about to turn on the burglar alarm and go upstairs when he noticed a light on in the back room. He went to check. Sitting on the sofa, looking for all the world as if she had spent the whole night crying, was Emma.

"What's wrong?" he asked, immediately sobering up as he raced to her side. "Have you been crying?"

Emma nodded. "I've been trying to call you all night!"

"Oh babe," said Ian as he remembered those missed calls. "It was noisy in the pub. I'm sorry. You know I'd never ignore you. Tell me sweetheart, what's the problem?"

"It's bad news," she said. "Really bad news . . . I've lost my job." And then she burst into tears.

Chapter 3

Emma was so upset that Ian didn't even bother trying to get any more detail out of her. Every time her sobs seemed to be on the verge of dying down, she would open her mouth, but before the words reached her lips another wave of sadness would crash over her. And she would be in tears again. Hugging her tight, Ian thought that the best he could do for now would be to stroke the top of her head, tell her everything would be all right and try not to yawn. Although he really needed to go to sleep, what he wanted more than anything else in the world was for Emma to be okay.

Ian and Emma had been together for seven years. They first came across each other back in their school days at St Benedict's in Smethwick. Ian was a couple of school years above Emma but had been on nodding terms with her because her brothers, Liam and Keith (the Kavanagh twins), were in the year above him. They had played five-a-side football with him over at Hadley Stadium.

Ian hadn't thought much about Emma back

then (mostly because the Kavanagh twins were big lads who didn't take kindly to people messing with their kid sister). Then, long after they had left school, he had bumped into her one Saturday morning on Bearwood High Street as she was coming out of Woolworths. Ian had recognised her straight away, even though she had changed quite a bit. While the schoolgirl Emma had been all NHS glasses and braces, the Emma now standing in front of him was stunning. She had beautiful green eyes, gorgeous long hair, a great smile and the most amazing laugh. It was like a cross between a chimp and an out of breath hyena, which some people might have found annoying. Ian thought it was the single best sound he had ever heard. Right there on the spot he had asked her if she fancied a drink in the King's Head across the road and Emma had agreed. A year or so later, in the middle of one of their many late-night talks, he told her that during that first drink it had taken him just ten minutes to realise how special she was. And a further twenty to realise that he never wanted to leave her side.

Ian looked down at Emma. Had she stopped crying? He wasn't sure.

"So what happened?" he asked.

Emma sat up and wiped her eyes on the back

of her hands. "I went into work as usual. Everything seemed normal and then just after five they started calling people into the office one by one. At first I thought maybe someone had been nicking money and they were trying to find out who had done it but then they called me. From the look on my line manager's face I knew that it wasn't anything to do with stealing. It was more serious than that."

"What did they say?"

"I can't remember. I wasn't listening properly, to be honest. I was too busy trying not to burst into tears on the spot. Anyway, the point is that the bank is cutting back on staff costs by thirty per cent and I'm one of the first to go. They were really nice about it. They've promised to give me a good reference and everything but I've no idea what I'm going to do. I've only ever had two jobs in my life and I really liked this one."

"Well, maybe this will be a good thing," said Ian. "It's not like you haven't talked about doing something else. A while back you were thinking about going to university. Maybe you should do that."

"That was all talk," sighed Emma. "I don't really want to go. I'd have to do an access course to start off with and I think they take a year or two. Then there would be another three years after that. I need money. *We* need money. Going to university just isn't an option right now."

"Well, what about a change in career then? You once told me that you quite fancied being a florist . . . or how about a beautician? The bathroom cabinet is stuffed with all your lotions and potions. Surely that will be enough for you to start your own beauty shop?"

Emma sniffed and smiled. "The way you go on about my make-up anyone would think that you don't like me looking pretty!"

"Listen, you," said Ian, grinning, "You could bin all your make-up and still be the best looking girl that I have ever met."

"Really?"

Ian nodded and kissed the top of her head. "By a mile."

"I love you, you know," said Emma.

"I know," said Ian. "I love you too."

Ian yawned widely and stretched his arms. "I'm really sorry, Ems. I do want to talk to you about this whole work thing, babe, but I'm shattered. Why don't we just head to bed and have a good night's sleep? Tomorrow I'll make you breakfast in bed and we can talk about it for as long as you like. How does that sound?"

Emma smiled, put her arms around Ian and kissed him. "That sounds brilliant. Do you know what? You are the best boyfriend in the entire world."

"I know," grinned Ian giving her a wink. "But don't go telling your mates, okay? Otherwise they'll all want a go!"

Chapter 4

It was just after eight as Ian got to his bus stop on the next Monday morning. Most of his usual fellow travellers were already there. There was the young woman with the green uniform, the middle-aged man who fell asleep in his seat and the young couple who always looked as if they were in the middle of a row. Every last one of them had a look that said, "How can it be Monday *already*?" Ian, however, was listening to a new album on his iPod and feeling glad that in a few moments he would be on the bus with nothing more pressing to do than look out of the window for the next twenty minutes. He had a look on his face that said, "It's Monday! Great! Bring it on!"

Ian went to his usual seat on the left-hand side of the middle part of the upper deck and sat down. As the bus pulled away he watched the world pass by through the window. He tried to lose himself in the music but kept being drawn back to thoughts about Emma and her current job situation.

Ian had tried hard to make Emma's weekend as

much fun as he could. On Saturday morning he had made her breakfast in bed as promised, then surprised her with a picnic tea in Lightwoods Park. In the evening he had taken her for a meal at a posh Japanese restaurant in The Mailbox shopping centre. On the Sunday morning he had treated her to brunch (even though he still wasn't quite sure what "brunch" was) at her favourite gastropub. In the afternoon he had invited all her family over for tea and even baked a cake. Finally, on Sunday evening, while Emma soaked in the bath that he had run for her, he had nipped out to Blockbusters and rented *two* films that featured Hugh Grant. He was Ian's least favourite actor in the entire world. Yes, Ian had without a doubt gone so far above and beyond the call of duty that even Emma's best friend Selina had joked that if Emma ever dumped him, she would snap him up in a second. So why did he still feel so down? Why did he feel as though he wanted to do more? The answer came just as the bus reached Five Ways. The reason he felt so bad was simple. He loved Emma. In fact he loved Emma in a way that men his age should only do if they keep it to themselves and don't make a big deal about it. So her unhappiness was now his unhappiness too.

****

Ian was still pondering what he was going to do about this when he saw Douglas, his line manager, standing in front of him.

"What's up, Doug? If you're after those figures you asked me for on Friday I'm still working on them."

"Nah," said Douglas in his usual matey manner, "I just want a quick word with you in my office."

Ian followed Douglas, wondering what was going on. Was he going to be sacked? Ian was pretty sure not. His last sackable offence had been well over a year ago and although it had involved a very slow afternoon, the world's largest ball of rubber bands and a trip to the eighteenth floor, this couldn't be about that. So what could it be?

"Take a seat," said Douglas as Ian came into his office and closed the door.

"What's all this about?" asked Ian.

Douglas laughed. "It's not bad news Ian, if that's what you're thinking! I just wanted a little chat, that's all."

"Okay," said Ian, shifting nervously in his seat.

Douglas leaned back in his chair and gave Ian a hard stare. "How long have you been here with us on the fourth floor, Ian?"

"Eight years."

"And do you like it?"

Ian nodded. "It's a good place to work."

"Could it be said that you like the fourth floor a bit too much?"

"In what way?"

Douglas held up his hand. "No need to worry, Ian, really there's no need. I'm just trying to get to the heart of what drives you."

"Drives me?"

"Yes, drives you."

"I'm not quite sure what you're on about, Douglas."

"Well, let me put it another way. In eight years you've never once applied for promotion."

"That's because I like my job."

"But don't you think you're wasting your talents? Everyone in the office thinks the world of you. There's no doubt in my mind that you could be a leader . . . So much so that I'd like you to consider putting your name forward for a job I have in mind."

"And which job would that be?" asked Ian, even though he had no wish to apply for a promotion.

"My job," said Douglas with a grin. "I want you to apply for the job of team leader."

Chapter 5

It was just after one in the afternoon. A stunned Ian was sitting in a bar on Broad Street sipping a pint of Guinness with his best friend and work mate, Amar, who was also stunned.

"I can't believe it mate," said Amar. "They want you to be team leader."

"I know," said Ian. "It's madness, isn't it? Why would they want me of all people? Do I look like a team leader to you?"

Amar laughed. "Not really."

"Exactly. I'm glad I'm not alone in seeing how daft this all is."

"I'm not saying it's daft," said Amar. "Just a bit of a surprise. But do you know what? Now that the idea is out there, I think it's a pretty good one. Everyone in the office likes you, you've worked there for years and, to top it all, you're great with people."

"I'm good at getting people up on dance floors, or staying for an extra pint, but getting people to work? No chance. This is mad."

"So what are you going to do? Say no? Now

Emma's out of a job won't you need the extra cash?"

"Emma won't be out of a job forever," said Ian firmly. "It'll be a couple of weeks tops so there won't be any need for me to do anything drastic. Nope, I can't see me accepting this job. No way."

"And what will Emma have to say when she finds out?"

"Oh, she'll be fine with it," said Ian. "Just fine."

****

"Are you insane?" barked Emma across the kitchen table when Ian told her about the job offer, as they sat eating pasta that evening.

"I thought you of all people would agree with me," said Ian. "You're always saying how I should do what makes me happy."

"Of course I am!" snapped Emma. "But only when you're talking about small things like whether you should bother going to football or have that extra slice of pizza. I think you should make yourself happy with things like that, but not big things like jobs! I've just lost mine in case you've forgotten. And we've got a little thing called a mortgage to pay in case it's slipped your mind. Before you say it's not just

21

about the money, you're right it's not just about the money. It's about pensions, and getting on in life, and starting a family. And, above all, us." She shook her head in disbelief. "Do you know what Ian? Sometimes I haven't got a clue what's going through your head!" She put down her knife and fork and fixed him with her hardest stare. "Just so that we both understand each other, let me say this as simply as I can. You are taking this job and that's that."

Later on, having had a chance to calm down a little as they sat on the sofa watching TV, Emma sighed and turned to face Ian.

"You do know that I'm only having a go about this job thing because I want what's best for you, don't you?"

Ian nodded. "I know you do, babe. It's just that . . ."

"What?"

"What if I don't like it?"

"Then you can do something else."

"But that's just it. I don't want to do anything else. I've got the perfect job. Okay, so it doesn't pay a huge amount of money but it does make me happy."

Emma looked at him for a minute and then smiled. "Fine," she said. "If it's going to make you miserable, don't take the job."

"Are you sure?"

She nodded. "Yeah, I'm sure. Anyway, when I got back from the job centre there was a message from one of the agencies that I signed up with telling me that they've a job that might be just up my street. I don't know what it is yet. It might come to nothing but you never know."

"It'll be all right," said Ian, putting his arm around Emma and pulling her close. "I'm sure this job is going to be the one for you. I've got a feeling about it. A really good feeling."

Next day Ian woke up feeling like a man who had just been let off the hook. Everything seemed brighter and more vivid. As he made his way to the bus stop it was all he could do to stop himself from grinning like an idiot at complete strangers.

Ian got into work just before nine. He made his way straight to his line manager's office and knocked on the door. Ian told Douglas that he had given the whole job promotion thing a lot of thought and that, although he was flattered, he had decided that he was really happy where he was for the time being. Douglas spent a good half an hour trying to persuade Ian that he was making a mistake but Ian wouldn't change his mind. He left Douglas's office feeling like a free man. He was so happy that the rest of the day went by in a flash and, as five o'clock approached, he decided he would treat Emma for being such a cool girlfriend. He got out his phone and called her.

"It's me," he said when she picked up. "Do you fancy meeting up in town for something to eat? My treat."

"That sounds great," said Emma, "because I'm in the mood for a bit of a party."

"Why?"

"Because I've got a job."

"That's fantastic!" said Ian. "I'm really chuffed for you sweetheart. Where is it?"

"Have a guess," said Emma.

"Fine," said Ian, even though he hated guessing games. "HSBC?"

"Nope," said Emma, "better than that."

"Okay," said Ian. "Selfridges. You spend a fortune in there so think of all the staff discount you'll be getting."

"Nope," said Emma, "this is way better than staff discounts."

"I give up," said Ian. "Come on, where is your new job?"

"The Policy Planning department of the Department of Work and Pensions in Birmingham!" she cried. "It's true, Ian! I've got a job in your office! You and I are going to be workmates!"

Chapter 6

It was the next morning and Ian was making his way to his usual bus stop on the Hagley Road. Even though it was meant to be summer, the sky above him was a deep, dark gun-metal grey. It was three-layers cold and the lack of office girls in skimpy tops on their way to work made him wonder if he had missed the memo about the entire season being cancelled. As it happened, a beautiful summer's day would have been completely wasted on Ian, given his current mood.

Although some fifteen hours had passed since Emma had broken the news that she would be temping in his office for a whole month, Ian was still finding it hard to come to terms with. He had put on a brave face as he took her out to Brindley Place for a drink and a bite to eat, and did his best to fuss over her and make it clear that he was really happy. But the truth was very different. He wasn't happy. He wasn't happy for her at all. The more she kept going on about how much fun it would be getting the bus to work together, having lunch together and getting to put names to all the faces of his work friends, the more Ian thought that this was the end of life as he knew it.

"You think I'm making too big a deal out of this don't you?" said Ian as he and Amar sat in the break room, each eating a bag of crisps. "You're thinking, 'Why's he moaning? It's not like she's going to be at the desk next to him watching his every move.'"

"You took the words right out of my mouth," said Amar through a mouthful of cheese and onion crisps. He swallowed and then poked his tongue around his mouth to clear up any bits. "Look mate," he said, "don't get me wrong, I do understand. If it was my missus coming to work here I'd top myself. I mean I love Rukmani to bits and I would lay down my life for her in a second but the woman never stops talking. From the moment I get in from work to the moment I leave, all she does is tell me a whole bunch of stuff I don't want to know! If you've been wondering what Rukmani's second cousin's next-door neighbour had for breakfast, I'm your man! If you want to know why the husband of the woman who sits at the cash desk next to Rukmani left her, I'm your man!"

"If you're desperate to hear what Rukmani's

old college friend Natasha is thinking of calling her new terrier puppies, I'm your man! Mate, if you want to know any bit of news about a whole bunch of people you've never met and would never hope to meet then, once again I'm your man. But I've met your missus. Emma's lovely. She's not a gob on legs like mine. So I don't quite see why the fact that she's temping here for a little while is such a huge deal."

"Because she's my girlfriend."

"And?"

"Well I already live with her. So if I start working with her too it'll mean I'll be spending twenty-four hours a day, seven days a week with her."

"So what?" said Amar, shrugging. "People do that all the time. Look at Steve and Annette in Bought Ledger. They live and work together."

"That's different. Steve and Annette met at work. The only version of Steve that Annette knew was Work Steve but Emma and I met out in the real world. She has no idea what Work Ian is like. She only knows Home Ian who is kind and lovely and all that."

"Well, maybe she'd like Work Ian if she met him."

Ian shook his head sadly. "No, mate, Emma

can never meet Work Ian. She'd hate him. She'd think he was a boorish, show-off boozer who spends too much money and a little too much time flirting with his boss's PA."

"So ditch Work Ian then."

"But I love Work Ian. Work Ian makes me happy. And anyway Home Ian only exists because I get to be Work Ian from Monday to Friday. If I have to spend the whole week being Home Ian, I'll die."

"Come off it, mate," snorted Amar. "It can't be that bad! Look, you need the money don't you?"

Ian nodded.

"And it's only for a bit, isn't it?"

Ian nodded again.

"And it's not like you can even stop her is it?"

Ian looked at the crisp packet in his hand. Could he stop her coming to work in his office by locking her in the bathroom? It was not a bad idea and, of course, he wouldn't leave her there. Even so, Ian was pretty sure that Emma would go mental. And if there was one thing worse than working with Emma, it was living with Emma when she was angry at him.

"No," he said, looking up at Amar, "it's not like I can actually stop her from doing anything."

"So the choice is she comes to work here and

you make the best of it, or she comes to work here and you make the worst of it?"

"Yeah," sighed Ian, "it's pretty much like that."

"So what's it going to be?"

"That," said Ian, "is a good question." He looked at his crisps and lost his appetite. "I don't know the answer. But I do know that the best thing right now is to go back to work."

Chapter 7

In the end, Ian decided to be as upbeat about Emma's new temp job as possible and hang on to the fact that she'd only be at Holling House for a month. Over the next few days he managed to convince himself that it wasn't such a big deal. He told himself it was a small deal, a very small deal indeed and before he knew it the whole thing would be over and he could go back to normal life. But then at ten minutes past eight on the following Monday morning, just as he had sat down on the loo for his usual ten minute thinking time, his mood was broken by Emma shouting up the stairs.

"Ian!"

Ian ignored her. It was an unwritten rule that he should never be disturbed whenever ten minutes past eight came and he headed to the loo for his ten minute "thinking time'. Up until now Emma had seemed to understand his need for both silence and regular bowel movements but now Ian wasn't so sure. Maybe in the excitement of her new job she had forgotten the rule. He decided to ignore her in the hope that she might realise her mistake on her own.

"Ian!"

One more chance.

"Iaaaaaaaaaaaaannnnnnn!"

Ian had no choice but to stop what he was doing, pull up his trousers and find out what she wanted.

"About time," said Emma, from the bottom of the stairs, with her coat on and her bag over her shoulder. "I thought you were never going to come out of there! Come on, slow coach, we need to get going."

"Going?" said Ian. "Going where?"

"Are you joking?" snapped Emma. "It's my first day at work, you idiot, and I don't want to be late."

"So?"

"So I want you to hurry up."

"But why?" As the words left his lips he saw what she was getting at. "You want us to go in together?"

"Well of course I do! I'm not going to turn up there on my own, am I?"

"Why not? You always turned up at the bank on your own."

Emma narrowed her eyes. "You can't mean it can you? Even though we'll both be working in the same office, you want me to make my own way there?"

"Of course not," said Ian, even though that was exactly what he had meant. "It's just that . . ."

"What?"

It was clear from her face that if he told Emma he needed a bit of peace and quiet on his way to work, she would go mad. He needed an excuse and he needed one quick. He found one at the end of his wrist.

"All I'm saying is that if we leave now we'll be too early," he said, waving his watch. "Think about it. It's only ten past eight, Ems! It takes exactly seven minutes to walk from ours to the bus stop. There's a bus every five minutes that can drop you off at Five Ways. It's a five-minute walk from the bus stop to Holling House. Then you've got a forty-two second wait for the lifts in reception and a thirty-eight second journey to the fourth floor once a lift arrives. If you leave now you'll be . . ." he did the sums in his head, ". . . a whole thirty-six and a half minutes early."

"I don't care about being early!" said Emma. "I only care about not being late, okay? So whatever it is you're doing in the bathroom just speed it up. I am not going to be late for my first day at work just because you take half an

32

hour to do what takes normal people two minutes!"

****

As Ian walked along with Emma to the bus stop he found his mind beginning to drift. It wasn't that he wasn't interested in what she was telling him about her friend Petra's relationships (although he wasn't). But Emma's new job had made him miss not only his ten minutes of loo-based "me-time" but also his seven minutes of iPod on his way to the bus stop. Worse, unless some kind of miracle was about to occur he would also miss out on a further fifteen minutes of iPod listening and staring blankly out of the bus window time, too. He looked at his watch. It wasn't even half-past eight and already Emma's new temp job had ruined his day. Really, he thought, as they waited for the number nine, how could this day get any worse? Fifteen minutes and a bus ride later, Ian found out the answer to his question.

"Where would you like me to sit?" asked Emma as Douglas finished the tour of the office right in front of Ian's desk.

"Now that," said Douglas, "is a good question. Free desk space is a bit short around here."

33

Ian looked at the free desk space next to his own. It had been empty ever since Colleen Newman had left to go travelling. He felt ill. Surely Douglas wouldn't do that to him would he? Not when there was a free desk next to Amar.

Choose Amar!

Choose Amar!

Choose Amar!

"How about there?" said Douglas, pointing to Colleen's old desk. "I'm sure Ian will make you feel right at home."

Chapter 8

"One o'clock!" said Emma breezily, looking at her watch. "I can't believe I've already done half a day's work. The time seems to have flown by, don't you think?"

"Oh yes," replied Ian, for whom the morning hadn't so much flown as sunk without a trace.

"So what are we doing for lunch?"

Lunch? thought Ian. *Isn't it enough that I had breakfast with you and will have dinner with you later? Now you've got to take away the only meal I don't eat sitting across from you?*

"Er . . . well me and Amar usually just nip over to Gregg's and bring something to eat at our desks."

"Sounds like a good plan," said Emma. "I'll walk up with you but I'm going to need some cash so I'll have to go over to the bank at some point."

Amar came over and started chatting to Emma and then the three of them wandered up to the shopping centre at Five Ways. Reaching the sandwich shop, Emma asked Ian to get her a prawn mayo roll and a bottle of water while she made her way over to HSBC.

"So how has it gone this morning?" asked Amar once Emma was out of earshot.

"Badly," said Ian as they got into the queue. "Very badly indeed."

Ian felt it was the single worst morning he had ever had at work. It wasn't that Emma had done anything wrong but the simple fact of her sitting next to him had killed his whole morning. "It's like when you're at school and you and your mates have been naughty, so the teacher splits you all up and one of you ends up sitting next to the class swot," he explained to Amar as they stood in line at Gregg's the Bakers. "Emma's the class swot and that means I can't have any fun."

Amar looked surprised. "She's stopping you having fun without saying a word? I take my hat off to her. My missus has to at least open her mouth to have that effect on me!"

"It must be some kind of Jedi mind trick," said Ian. "All morning I could feel myself repeating the words, 'My name is Ian Greening and I will not have any fun at all today.' And guess what? It's worked. I didn't get to finish the Monday morning joke email, or sort out a venue for Chris in Bought Ledger's leaving do. I didn't even add the half a dozen rubber bands that came with the mail this morning to our ever-growing rubber band ball. In fact I haven't had a single laugh all day."

"So what are you going to do?" asked Amar. "Get her to sit somewhere else?"

"Oh yeah," replied Ian. "I can really see that happening, can't you? 'Ems, you know how you're sitting at the desk right next to me? Well, as it turns out, it's putting me off my game so could you do me a favour and sit somewhere else?' My life wouldn't be worth living. Why couldn't Douglas have put her next to you?"

"No, no, no," said Amar shaking his head. "I don't need her sitting next to me. Don't forget Emma and Rukmani are Facebook friends. I can't have your missus reporting my every move back to mine . . . even if it does save your skin."

"Still, better you than me though, eh?" said Ian with a grin as he reached the front of the queue.

Amar frowned. "What does that mean?"

"That, my friend, means you'd better get used to the idea of toning down work larks. I've got a strong feeling that once I've used my gift of the gab on Douglas, you'll find yourself lumped with a brand new desk buddy."

****

"No," said Douglas.

"But you don't even know what I'm going to ask," said Ian.

"You're going to ask me if I can move the new temp – who funnily enough I didn't even know was your girlfriend until Amar told me five minutes ago – to a new desk."

"But—"

"Listen, Ian," said Douglas. "I'd love to help you out but the truth of the matter is that I couldn't move her even if I wanted to. I'd never hear the end of it if Emma complained to Human Resources that she was made to move desks just because her boyfriend didn't like it. As much as I like you, mate, I can't really get involved in stuff like this. Just think," smiled Douglas, "if you had agreed to take my job, you'd have my lovely office with its own closing door all to yourself."

"Oh, come on Doug," whined Ian. "There's got to be something you can do. How would you like it if I plonked your wife in the desk next to you all day?"

"I'd love it," said Douglas. "I don't see enough of her as it is."

"And that's all you've got to say?"

"Pretty much," replied Douglas. "You have a good day now, won't you?"

"Yeah," replied Ian. "I'm sure it'll be a barrel of laughs."

Chapter 9

Ian's first afternoon working with Emma was, if anything, worse than the morning. Usually the afternoon was Ian's favourite part of the day. Most of his friends who had actual work to do would have had the bulk of it done by this time and would be more open to having a laugh, but as he looked around the office most people seemed genuinely busy. This was fine today, because he had something on his mind and for once it wasn't Emma, it was a large brown folder.

The Regional Study folder had been sitting on the edge of his desk for a good ten minutes now, ever since Douglas had given him strict instructions about what he was to do with it. The first part was to hand over the folder to one of the Admin girls. The second was to explain the parts of the folder that needed explaining. And the third was getting the girls to type up the article, copy it and pass it on to all department heads by the end of the day. On any other day of the week (or at least any other day without Emma being in this office) this would have been a pleasure. But today (and indeed any day that had his girlfriend sitting less than six inches away from his elbow) it was going to be a nightmare.

The girls in Admin (or as they liked to be known, "the Ad Girls") were easily the hottest girls on the entire fourth floor. No one had ever quite worked out why Admin always seemed to attract the best looking women, but no one really cared about the answer. "It's like asking a weather man why it's a sunny day," Ian had said to Amar when the topic came up. "The fact of the matter is, no one cares why it's a sunny day when it's a sunny day. All that matters when it's a sunny day is that you go outside as much as possible and enjoy it."

There were three Admin girls in total. Jodie, Danni (Ian's favourite) and Sam. The girls were all in their early twenties and although they had many things in common (*Heat* magazine and a fondness for hair extensions, for example), there was one thing that truly united them. The fact that they all thought Ian was the most fanciable guy on the fourth floor. Ian knew that being "the most fanciable guy on the fourth floor" was not much to feel big-headed about. But even though he would never have cheated on Emma in a million years, it gave him a warm glow inside.

While Emma wasn't the jealous type, this didn't mean she wouldn't make his life a living hell should she suspect that he spent his afternoons at work being witty and charming for the Ad Girls.

Which was worse? wondered Ian. To fall out with your boss for the second time in a day because you hadn't done your job or fall out with your girlfriend because she thought you were a cheating scumbag? It really was a lose/lose situation unless he could come up with a way out. Suddenly it came to him. The perfect plan that would allow him to talk to the Admin girls without Emma suspecting a thing.

"I'm gasping," said Ian, standing up. "I'm going to make myself a brew. Fancy one Em?"

Emma shook her head. "I'm off tea at the minute. I saw something in the paper last week about how too much tannin isn't good for you."

"Okay," said Ian, not to be defeated. "How about a glass of water? You're supposed to drink two litres a day aren't you? I've barely seen you drink a drop."

Emma shook her head again. "I know you're right but I'm not in the mood for water today."

"But a glass of water drunk every hour keeps your brain ticking over."

"My brain's just fine, thank you," laughed Emma. "What about you though? You never drink water at home. Your kidneys must look like a pair of dried up old prunes."

"They're fine," said Ian swiftly. "Okay, so you don't want tea or water and it's too early for a white wine, so how about . . . a diet Coke?"

"Now that," said Emma, "would be perfect."

For forty-five minutes after his return from the shop to get Emma's giant bottle of diet Coke, Ian sat willing his girlfriend to go to the loo so that he could talk to the Admin girls. But Emma must have a bladder the size of a football because even after an hour she hadn't made a move towards the loo.

"You seem a bit thoughtful," said Emma, nudging him with her elbow. "There's no need to spend the afternoon dreaming about me when I'm right here next to you!"

"You'll never believe this," said Ian, "but I really was thinking about you. I was just wondering whether you'd been to the loo at all today."

"Why would you wonder that of all things?"

"Because I thought you might not know where they are and be too shy to ask."

"They're on the second floor," said Emma. "I found them this morning. And to answer your question, yes, I have been to the loo."

"Good," said Ian. "But how about this afternoon? I only ask because I'm pretty sure I read in the paper that people don't go to the loo enough these days."

"I go to the loo plenty thank you."

"So why don't you go now?"

"Because I don't want to."

"Are you sure?"

"Yes, I'm sure."

"But are you sure you're sure? You know how it is. Sometimes you never really know you need the loo until you think about it."

Emma looked at him. "Have you gone mad? What's all this wee talk about?"

"Fine. Don't go to the loo if you don't want to. I was just looking out for you that's all." He realised that all this talk of needing the loo had made him need the loo. Urgently. With a heavy heart and a full bladder he rose to his feet.

"Where are you going?" asked Emma.

"To the loo," he said.

"Hmm," said Emma, rising to her feet. "Now I think about it, maybe I do need the loo after all. Let's go together."

Chapter 10

It was just after six on a Friday morning four weeks later and Ian was lying awake in bed next to Emma with a huge grin on his face. Today was Emma's last day temping in his office. Ian was so excited that every now and again he let out a silent, "Yeeeeeeeeeeesssssssssssssss!" through gritted teeth. Was this what Geoff Hurst felt like when he heard the final whistle, playing against Germany back in 1966? Ian thought so because right now he was sure that life couldn't get any better.

For this past month, working with Emma day in and day out had been the hardest thing Ian had ever done in his life. Every day he had gone to work hoping that today might be better than yesterday. And every day he had come home disappointed.

On the second day, Emma said that they were spending too much money on pre-packed sandwiches and so, much to his friend's amusement, she made him share a pasta salad and bottle of mineral water at her desk. On the fourth day, Ian had hoped to get drunk at Trevor from Strategy Planning's leaving do. But Emma gave him so many disapproving looks that he gave up on beer and drank orange juice for the rest of the night. On the sixth day, Emma brought in the cute cat photo calendar that he hated from home and put it on her desk. Right in his eye line.

On the eighth day, Emma made friends with the Admin girls after a Health and Safety meeting. Now they had all stopped flirting with him. On the tenth day, Emma decided that every other lunchtime they would go for a walk to spend some quality time together out of the office. On the twelfth day, Emma found Ian and Amar's secret napping place in the store cupboard at the back of the break room and banned them both from ever going there again.

On the fourteenth day, Emma started a book club and so far had made him spend two precious lunchtimes in the fourth floor meeting room talking about boring books that made his head ache. On the sixteenth day, Emma talked him into coming in to work on casual Friday wearing a vile purple shirt she had bought him on his birthday. And on the eighteenth day, when Ian was going to call in sick because he'd finally had enough, Emma begged him come to work because she didn't want to spend all day on her own. But now, on this the twentieth and final day of Emma's temping, the end was in sight. He just had to get through this final day and everything would be okay.

****

The first sign that everything wasn't going to be okay came at just after midday. Ian's boss, Douglas, poked his head out of the door to his office and asked Emma to come in for a quick chat. The second sign that everything wasn't going to be okay came five minutes later, when Ian heard Emma's joyful cackle. It sounded as though she had just heard the funniest joke in the world. But the third and final sign that everything wasn't going to be okay came just after twenty past twelve when, beaming from ear to ear, Emma came out of her meeting with Douglas. She was calling over her shoulder as she left, "Of course. Just give me lunchtime to think about it and I'll have an answer for you this afternoon."

"Okay," said Ian as Emma got back to her desk and took her seat. "What's going on?"

"Nothing much," said Emma grinning.

"Oh, Em, don't make me beg will you? It's

clear from that cheesy grin that something is up, so what is it? "

"Douglas has just offered me a job!" said Emma clapping her hands with glee. "Can you believe it, Ian? We're going to be desk buddies for life!"

Ian swallowed hard. "So you've said yes?"

"I told him I'd talk it over with you."

"Why would you tell him that?" asked Ian.

"Because this was only ever supposed to be a temp job. It's been fun but part of me wonders whether, you know, if I worked here full-time, I might feel a little bit hemmed in by you."

"By me?"

Emma nodded. Ian breathed a huge (but hidden) sigh of relief. "Sweetie," he said, "there is no way I'd ever want you to feel hemmed in. So if you don't think you ought to take the job, then don't take it."

"But that's the thing," said Emma. "Deep down I really do want to take it."

"But what about the hemmed-in feeling?"

Emma shrugged. "I think I could get used to it. I mean, I've been here a month and you haven't felt hemmed in by me, have you?"

Ian thought about telling Emma exactly how hemmed in he felt but at the last moment he stopped. Emma was so happy, he just couldn't bring himself to ruin things for her. This was no time for the truth. "I've loved it," he said and kissed her on the cheek. "It really has made my month having you around."

"Well in that case," said Emma rising to her feet, "there's no point in me hanging about, is there? I'll tell Doug yes right now."

As Ian watched Emma cross the room to Douglas's office, two thoughts popped into his head. The first was that he loved Emma more than he had ever loved any woman in his life. The second was that the idea of working with her forever made him want to poke his eyes out with the wrong end of a spoon. There was no way that he could stand working with her every day. No way at all. He would have to do something about it and he was going to have to do it soon or risk never being happy at work or at home ever again.

Chapter 11

Emma had a stunned look on her face.

"What did you just say?"

"I said, I think it's time we started a family," said Ian, barely able to believe that he had said the words himself.

"Are you serious?"

"Completely serious. I love you. We've been together ages. And I think it's time."

"But I don't understand," said Emma. "Where's all this come from? Last time I checked, weren't you the man who said I'd got more chance of talking you into a sex change than a baby?"

"Times change," said Ian. "Sometimes a man's got to do what a man's got to do."

The reason why this man was doing what he was doing had very little to do with wanting his own small bundle of joy. Since Emma had started working permanently at the Policy Planning department over a month ago, every single one of his attempts to get her to leave had failed.

So far he had tried:

1. Secretly signing Emma up on recruitment websites in the hope that one of them might offer her a job back in banking.
2. Suggesting to her that she really ought to leave work and do an access course so that she could go to university and get a degree.
3. Attempting to convince her after an evening of SingStar that she had a great voice and that she should leave work and put all her efforts into getting onto *X-Factor*.
4. Moving objects on her desk when she wasn't looking and then telling her it was the work of the office poltergeist.
5. Hiding all her work clothes and then denying knowing anything about it when she found them under the bed in the spare bedroom.
6. Introducing her to Keith on Reception in the hope that having daily talks with the world's most boring man would make her think twice about coming to work.
7. Writing her letters from a secret office admirer called "Mr X" whose all-time favourite film was *Police Academy 5*,

which he claimed to have seen 2,388 times.

8. Buying her a copy of the *Rough Guide to Australia* and suggesting that they both leave work and go travelling.

9. Turning off the air conditioning in the office on the warmest day of the year so far.

10. Getting his mate Tom in the Advance Planning Team to call Emma up for a fake interview for a fake job on the eighth floor in the hope that it might inspire her to think about other jobs.

When Emma turned down the fake job – by telling her fake interviewer that that she couldn't leave the fourth floor because she was having such a good time working with her boyfriend – Ian decided to pull out the big guns. And ask Emma if she wanted to start a family.

"You do realise that this is the single maddest thing you have ever done?" said Amar once Ian had finished telling him the plan. "How can you think it's okay to bring a child into the world just so that you don't have to work with your missus? I mean, what are you going to tell the little nipper when he's older and asks you why you wanted a baby? You'll be kissing any half-decent

Father's Day presents goodbye if he finds out the answer is 'because your mum was driving me crazy.' Mate, I know this is a great place to work but why don't you just get another job?"

"Because I like this job and I saw it first," whined Ian.

"You sound like a big baby . . . Oh, wait a second. You're not the baby here, are you? That's right, you're going to make one instead, just so you don't have to sit next to your girlfriend day in day out."

"Okay," snapped Ian. "You tell me what I should do. I love this job and I love Emma. Now, because of a whole bunch of stuff outside my control, I have to choose between being with Emma but unhappy at work or being at work but unhappy without Emma. Because you know what? She will leave me if I tell her that I can't stand working with her. She'd never forgive me in a million years."

"So the answer is to have a baby is it?"

Ian looked down at his shoes. "No, of course it isn't."

"Good lad," said Amar. "You know it makes sense."

****

Later that day, having just got back from his second trip of the afternoon to the shop for a packet of crisps, Ian sat down and looked at Emma.

"Babe," he began, "you know all that stuff I said this morning about wanting to start a family? I know you said you'd think about it but . . ."

Emma smiled and put a finger up to his lips. "You don't need to say a single word, sweetheart. I know what you're going to say and I feel it too. Of course we want kids but now's not the right time is it?" Emma took hold of Ian's hand. "Are you okay?"

"Yeah, of course I am," he lied. "Why wouldn't I be?"

"It's just that lately I've been feeling like you're really unsettled. This past month or so all you've done is think about our future. Is there something bothering you? Because if there is, you know you can tell me."

Ian knew he should tell her what was really wrong but he couldn't find the right words. So he said something else that had been on his mind.

"As it happens there is," said Ian quietly. "Will you marry me?"

"Yes," she said, without missing a beat. "Right now I can't think of a thing I'd like to do more."

Chapter 12

The effect of the engagement was that for a couple of weeks Ian was so blissfully happy that Emma could do no wrong. Getting back late to the office from an all day inter-agency meeting he found that she had tidied his entire desk. Did he get angry that he couldn't find anything? No, he just laughed, told her he had been meaning to tidy it for some time and kissed her.

A few days later he noticed that every time he saw one of the Ad Girls they burst out laughing. Then he found out Emma had told them that when he was feeling stressed he liked to slap on one of her face masks, hop in the bath and read the latest issue of *Glamour*. Did Ian get mad? No, he just laughed, told the Ad Girls that even he had a girly side and kissed Emma. A week later Emma managed to convince the Out of Office Hours Social Committee that instead of bowling, followed by Nando's, followed by 2-for-1 cocktails in Henry J. Beans (like they did every month) they should go and see *Mamma Mia* at the Alexandra Theatre. Did Ian scream at the top of his voice that he didn't like musicals and certainly not with Abba songs? No, he just laughed, sang a couple of lines from *"Gimme! Gimme! Gimme! (A Man after Midnight)"* and kissed her. But then one day Emma did something so terrible that he couldn't laugh about it, find a witty line or even kiss her.

The Annual Policy Planning Department Away Day was Ian's favourite day of the year. He knew it was crazy but, secretly, he loved it more than Christmas. He loved it more than New Year's Eve. In fact Ian loved it more than Christmas and New Year's Eve rolled into one. On the surface it was an overnight stay in a posh seaside hotel for twenty-four hours of team-building, workshops and the odd lecture from a government minister. The truth of the matter was that it pretty much always ended up being one long party.

In previous years, Ian had seen senior managers getting off with waitresses at the hotel and Amar being sick out of the window of a sixth floor hotel room. Then there was the year a middle-aged woman from Bought Ledger streaked naked through the hotel lobby screaming, "Look at me! I'm a fairy!"

In the past six years alone they had been banned from three different venues in

Bournemouth, had an official telling off from a junior minister and once even made the front page of a local newspaper.

This year was meant to be the best year ever by a mile. Amar and the Ad Girls missed all the workshops and spent all day on the beach. The department director and a member of Senior Management got into a yelling match in the hotel lobby. Two members of the strategy team were sent home early for crimes so awful no one would even say what they were. And half of the Forward Planning Team were told they would be getting written warnings after a party in a fourth-floor bedroom that didn't finish until the police arrived at just after eight in the morning. It really was an Away Day to beat all other Away Days.

Not for Ian though. He missed the beach because Emma wouldn't skip any of the workshops. He missed the two members of the strategy team being sent home because at the time Emma wanted a cuddle on the bed while watching *Neighbours*. And he missed the Forward Planning Team's all-night party because right after dinner, as everyone was getting ready to hit the bars of Bournemouth, Emma asked Ian to come back to the room because she had a headache. That was the last straw. He could put up with a lot from Emma but not spoiling his last night in Bournemouth. Worse, having made him promise not to leave her alone, she had promptly fallen asleep.

The next morning Ian was still angry. And the following night too. But when he woke up the third morning at six and found his anger still there, he knew he had to do something. Part of him knew the sensible thing was to talk to Emma but now he was not only scared of hurting her, he was furious with her. He wasn't thinking straight. So he got up quietly, headed to the spare bedroom, opened up his laptop and began searching around the internet.

Later that day, when Emma headed to the break room to get her Pret-a-Manger salad from the office fridge, Ian leapt into her seat. He disabled her computer's firewall like his friend Stewart in IT had shown him, loaded up the image from his pen drive as an email attachment and pressed send. As quickly as he could, he put the firewall back, took out the pen drive and set Emma's computer back to sleep.

For a moment or two Ian could hear nothing but the beat of his own heart. He felt breathless and like he might actually faint. As soon as he had done it, he knew that it was not only wrong but pretty much evil. In a bid to clear his mind he went to the loo and splashed water on his face. It didn't help. He realised that he had gone too far. What he had done was too awful. He would have to go up to Stewart in IT and see if he could get the email back or at the very least hide where it had come from. Glad that he had made up his mind to do the right thing, he went back to the office but it was too late. Emma was standing at her computer in tears while an angry looking Douglas stood next to her shouting into his phone for IT to come up to the fourth floor right now.

Chapter 13

"This has been the worst day of my life! The worst ever," sobbed Emma as she and Ian got home and she flung herself on the sofa. "They're going to sack me for sure and I'll never be able to get another half-decent job again and all for something I didn't do! It's not fair, Ian! It's just not fair!"

"You never know," Ian said soothingly, "they might just give you a good telling off and leave it at that."

"But I haven't even done anything to be told off for!" sobbed Emma. "You know me. You know I'd never do what they say I've done. So who is picking on me? What have I done to make someone hate me so much that they would set me up like this?"

If it had been possible to press a button to open a door so he could jump in and be swallowed up, Ian would have been pressing it now. He hated seeing Emma upset like this. And he hated himself for putting her in this position in the first place.

The idea had come to him that morning. The only way to end the nightmare was to get Emma sacked. Heading to the spare room he had typed, "Reasons why people get sacked" into the search engine. One of the top entries was a story about an office worker who had forwarded a picture of a semi-naked glamour model with his boss's face stuck on her body. A few clicks and a cut and paste job later, Ian had exactly what he needed – Douglas's head stuck on the body of a topless girl on a Harley Davidson. Adding a speech bubble to the picture that said, "My name's Douglas and I like a big Chopper!" Ian had then downloaded the image on to his pen drive and put his plan in motion.

Watching Emma sobbing as IT took away her computer had been awful. She was sent home and told to come back first thing next morning to find out what would be happening to her. Feeling like he was going to throw up, Ian had asked Douglas for a half-day to go and look after her. It took a while to talk him into it but after ten minutes of begging, Douglas had finally said yes.

****

The next morning Ian still felt sick. Emma had spent most of the night crying and had even said she might not bother to go in as there was no point if all they were going to do was sack her.

"You never know," said Ian as Emma finally got up to take a shower. "Maybe they'll find out who really did it. Or maybe the person who did do it will own up."

"Do you really think that's likely?" sniffed Emma. "Come on, Ian. The kind of person who would sneak around using other people's computers like that is hardly likely to have the guts to own up, are they?"

Ian shook his head sadly. "No," he said. "They probably aren't."

Emma barely spoke a word on the way into work. She sat on the bus with her head against the window staring out into the traffic. Arriving at the office at five to nine, Emma was met at the door by Douglas. Without even a hint of a smile he led her to a room in which four members of Senior Management were seated, and closed the door.

"This is mad!" said Amar sitting down on the edge of Ian's desk. "Everyone knows that Emma would never do what they say she's done."

"You don't need to tell me that," said Ian. "What do you think will happen? A slap on the wrist?"

"More like a punch in the face, mate," said Amar. "If there's one thing they hate in the Civil Service it's people messing about with the internet at work. Add to that the fact it was a picture of a manager stuck on the body of a nudie model and I don't see how it can help being the sack."

"What if she got the union involved?"

"Is she even a member of the union?"

Ian shook his head. "The papers you've got to sign for the direct debits are still on the kitchen table."

"Then that's it," said Amar. "Game over."

****

An hour later the door to Douglas's office opened and Emma came out in tears.

"What happened?" asked Ian. "What did they say?"

"I have to leave immediately," said Emma. "My contract has been cancelled."

"They can't do that," said Ian. "Not for one lousy email!"

"They can," said Emma, "and they have." She looked up at Ian and shook her head. "Do you want to know what the worst thing about all this is? I never really wanted to take this stupid job in the first place. I thought the pressure of us spending so much time together would mean we'd end up fighting all the time, but it never happened. You were always so sweet and kind to me. You never made me feel like I was in the way. You always made me feel welcome. And although I won't miss the job, I'll miss you, Ian Greening. I'll miss you every minute."

Chapter 14

This time, Douglas wouldn't let Ian go home with Emma no matter how much he pleaded, so he had no choice but to say goodbye to Emma in the downstairs lobby.

"Everything will be all right," said Ian hugging her. "It will, really, babe. This was a rubbish job anyway. You'll get a better one. Just you wait and see. Then you'll look back on this moment and wonder what the fuss was about."

Emma nodded and kissed him, but he could tell that she didn't believe a word he said. She was worried about money. She was worried about finding another job. But most of all she was worried that getting sacked would stop her from ever getting a decent job ever again.

"Text me if you need anything," said Ian, feeling like the lowest of the low. "Anything at all. Just let me know and I'll sort it out for you straight away."

"I'll be fine," said Emma trying to put on a brave face. "You just make sure that you work as hard as you can today. The last thing we need is you getting sacked!"

For the rest of the day Ian stared blankly at Emma's empty chair wishing that he could turn back time. If only he could take back his actions and stop this terrible thing. What had been going through his mind? How did Emma deserve this? How could he ever look her in the eye when he had been the cause of so much pain? Ian wished he had never heard of the fourth floor of the Department of Work and Pensions. And even though he had got what he had wanted, now there was no way he could enjoy a single moment at work, knowing what the true cost of his actions had been. Life as he knew it was over. There was no chance of getting it back.

He picked up Emma's cat calendar. The picture for the month was of a tiny grey kitten, all soft fur and big eyes, poking its head out of a box. At any other time this photo would have made Ian pull a face in disgust. Today it made him smile, and feel sad, and miss Emma more than he thought he could.

He pulled out his phone and typed out a text. "Babe just want to say how much I love you. Things will be OK I promise." He pressed send. Then he put his phone away, took a deep breath, opened up a brand new spreadsheet and started typing.

****

Just before five, Ian was about to close down his computer, collect his things and head home when Amar appeared at his desk.

"Do you want to go for a drink?" he asked. "Just a quick one before you go home? Today must have really done your head in mate."

"I can't," said Ian. "I said to Emma I'd go straight home."

"Of course," said Amar. "You should be there for her. Are you going right now? I'm pretty much done for the day. Just give me a second and I'll walk up to the bus stop with you."

The pavement outside the office was busy with hundreds of workers making their way home. Ian and Amar stood on the steps in front of the lobby doors watching everyone walk by.

"Do you think any of these people like their jobs as much as we do?" asked Ian.

"I doubt it," said Amar. "Most people I know who work in offices say what they do is just a way to earn money. Nothing more and nothing less."

"But it's not like that at our place, is it?" said Ian. "We don't just do this for the money. If we did, I would have left a long time ago."

"You're right," said Amar. "It's about the people. It's about the fact that we can have a laugh. That somehow we seem to have found ourselves in a job where you look forward to coming in every day."

Ian's eyes were fixed on the ground. "It was me who sent the email from Emma's computer."

"I guessed it might have been," said Amar, staring straight ahead of him, "but I was sort of hoping I was wrong."

"Because I overstepped the mark?"

Amar put a hand on his friend's shoulder. "You don't need me to tell you what you've done and you don't need me to tell you what you're going to do about it."

"I know," said Ian. "But she'll leave me if I do."

"That's true, she might," said Amar. "But have you got any choice? If you're thinking the guilt is going to melt away, you're wrong. With things like this, stuff always gets a lot worse before it gets better. This way at least you know that you did the right thing."

"The right thing would be not to have done it at all."

"True again," said Amar. "But since your name isn't Dr Who and you haven't got a TARDIS to take you back in time, I'm guessing that you'll have to settle for telling the truth instead.'

Chapter 15

Standing at his front door, Ian reached into his trouser pocket, pulled out his house keys and was about to open the lock when he froze. His eyes flicked back and forth from the lock to his keys a few times until at last he closed his eyes and lowered his hand. The second he opened the door, life as he knew it would be over. Nothing would ever be the same again. Everything he cared about would be destroyed.

Ian wanted to run away or hide until he was feeling stronger. Would it make things worse if he turned round and went to the pub and told Emma everything when less sober? Wouldn't the result be the same? After all, she was going to leave him. He'd thought it through. He'd looked at things a million ways and in every one of them there was only one thing Emma *could* do.

Even if he didn't go to the pub, maybe he could just not bother going home? He could call Amar and ask to sleep on his sofa tonight and then speak to Emma on the phone. Telling her what he had done wouldn't be half as bad if he couldn't see her face. He didn't want to see her tears. He didn't want to see the hurt in her eyes. He didn't want to see anything to remind him that he had let down a girl who, only a few days earlier, had said to her mum he was "the most perfect man in the world."

Ian took a deep breath and this time his keys made it to the lock. He called out Emma's name and she called back from the bathroom.

"I'm in the bath," she yelled. "Be down in a sec, okay?"

Ian went into the kitchen, poured himself a glass of water and sat down at the table. He gulped down the water in a few seconds, put the empty glass on the table and looked around the room. The kitchen cupboards looked shabby and worn. Emma had wanted a new kitchen for ages and every other weekend a kitchen catalogue would appear on the table. Ian had promised only last week that come Christmas, once he'd got his credit card paid off, they would start saving for a brand new one. The news had made her so happy that it had been the only thing she talked about all day. Ian loved seeing her happy. The thought that he was only minutes away from making her desperately miserable made him wonder whether she would feel like he had never loved her at all.

"Hey, you," said Emma as she came into the kitchen in a towel. She sat on his lap and gave him a long slow kiss.

"What's that for?" asked Ian. "It's not my birthday is it?"

Emma tutted. "No stupid," she said, "you got that because a few things are clear to me now."

"Oh yeah," said Ian. "Like what?"

"Like the fact that none of this matters as long as I've got you. Like the fact that, even without a job, I'm still the luckiest girl in the world because we're getting married. And like the fact that some people spend their whole lives looking for what I've got with you and never find it." Emma put her arms around Ian and hugged him tightly. "Ian Greening. You are the finest man to ever walk this planet and I love you with my whole heart and will carry on loving you until the end of time." Emma put her damp head on his chest. "And that, young man, is what I have spent all day thinking."

Ian wanted to die. He really did. Was there any point in carrying on living after this? Right now he had the love of a good woman who thought he was the best thing since sliced bread. The minute he opened his mouth he would lose everything and every last good memory Emma had of him would be spoilt forever. Death compared to this would be far easier.

"Em," said Ian, sitting up in his chair. "Can you just take a seat please? I've got something I need to tell you."

"Oooh!" joked Emma, "This sounds interesting! You haven't got me the diamond ring we looked at last weekend, have you?"

"No," said Ian. "It's got nothing to do with rings."

"What about shoes?" said Emma. "I know I said I'd love those Dolce & Gabbana heels for my birthday, but you do know I was only joking don't you?"

"No," said Ian, "this isn't about shoes either."

"Okay, okay," said Emma. "It's not rings or shoes, so what is it?" Emma's face lit up as a thought popped into her head. "It's not the new kitchen is it? You've ordered it as a surprise haven't you? When are they coming to fit it?"

"Emma," said Ian. "This isn't about shoes and it isn't about rings or new kitchens either."

"Okay," said Emma.

"It's about me," said Ian, "and the fact that I've done the worst thing in the world."

And then Ian told her everything.

Chapter 16

"I can't believe it," said Emma as Ian finished confessing what he had done to her. "I really can't believe it."

"For what it's worth, I'm really sorry, Em, believe me. If I could have my time again I would never have done it. Honestly, it's the most stupid and hurtful thing that I've ever done."

"Stupid doesn't even cover the half of it!" said Emma. "You've made me look like a fool! There's me telling all my friends what a great guy you are and how you'd do anything for me when all this time you were plotting behind my back to get rid of me."

"It wasn't like that Em, honest. I just wasn't thinking straight that's all."

"And I'm guessing you blame me for that too!" Emma shook her head. "It's hard to know which is worse," she said quietly. "That you went out of your way to get me sacked or the fact that you hated working with me so much that you wanted to get rid of me. That's right, isn't it? You would've done anything to get rid of me, wouldn't you?"

Ian shook his head. "It wasn't like that, babe. You have to believe me."

"Okay then," said Emma. "Tell me what it was like. Tell me why it was so awful working day in, day out with your girlfriend!"

"You're getting it all wrong," said Ian. "The problem was with me not you."

"Are you really trying to palm me off with that rubbish?" snapped Emma. "Do you really think you can get away with using a line like, 'It's not you, it's me?' Of course it was you, Ian! I'm not the one who's been a lying, cowardly, sneaky little toad here! I'm not the one who didn't have the guts to have a simple talk with his girlfriend and I'm certainly not the one who got me sacked!"

"I know," said Ian. "I'm sorry, Emma, I'm really sorry."

He reached to touch her arm but she pushed him away.

"Don't touch me!" she snapped. "Don't you dare touch me again! You've hurt me, Ian. You've hurt me so much that I'm not sure things can ever be the same. You were the closest person to me in the world and you let me down, and all for what? So that you can have a laugh with your mates in a stupid job that you care about more than you do me? How can I not be insulted by that? How can I not think that this shows how little you care for me?"

"Listen, Em," said Ian, "you're getting the wrong end of the stick. It was never about making you look stupid. It really was about me and my problems. I should've said right from the start that I wasn't happy about you working at my place but I couldn't think how to do it without hurting your feelings."

"So let me get this straight: you didn't have the guts to talk to me about working at your place, but you had the guts to sneak onto my computer and send an email that got me sacked in front of the whole office? Have you any idea how shaming that was? How awful it felt thinking that someone in the office hated me so much that they would do that?"

"It was never meant to go this far," said Ian.

"But it did," said Emma, "and now that it's all out in the open we've both got to learn to live with what happens next."

Ian felt himself begin to panic. It was really going to happen, his worst nightmare. Emma was going to dump him. "You're not saying that you want to split up over this are you? I made a mistake, I admit that, and I promise you that I will make it up to you but please, Em, please don't split up with me. Not over this. It was stupid, that's all, just a stupid mistake and I'll never do anything like it again."

"Those are just words," said Emma rising to her feet. "You might mean them, you might not, and I will never know. But when it comes to love, what really counts is deeds. The things you do and the reasons why you do them. By acting the way that you have you've shown me that I don't matter to you. So maybe it's my turn to show you just how much you have hurt me. If you have any love for me at all, you will pack a bag and just go, Ian. Go and leave me alone."

"Go?" said Ian. "Go where?"

"To your mum and dad's . . . to Amar and Rukmani's . . . you could camp out right in the middle of your beloved office for all I bloody care! All I want is for you to go."

"But this is just for now, isn't it?" said Ian quickly. "Just so that you can sort your head out? You have to promise me you aren't ending it for good, Em. You have to promise that this isn't us breaking up forever."

Emma shook her head. "I can't make you that promise," she said, not looking at him. "I really can't, Ian. Because, right now, I just don't know."

Chapter 17

It was nearly a week later and Ian was at his desk. He was preparing some data for a seminar on future funding for the department when Amar appeared at his desk.

"Coming for lunch?"

Ian shook his head. "Nah, I think I'm going to give it a miss. I want to get these figures done before the end of the day."

"You do realise that you've worked through lunch every day this week, don't you mate?"

"I've got a lot to do."

Amar shook his head. "That might well be, but we both know what's going on here. Look, I'm going back to my desk to get my jacket and then I'm going to come back and you and I are going to have a drink. No excuses, okay?"

"Whatever," sighed Ian, turning off his computer. "I'm past caring about any of this anyway."

Minutes later, Ian and Amar made their way up to the Sports Café on Broad Street, where he ordered a bitter shandy for himself and a pint of Coke for Amar together with two packets of salt and vinegar crisps.

"So how's living at your mum and dad's house going?" said Amar, his mouth full of one of the ice cubes from his drink.

"It's great," said Ian. "I love it."

Amar looked surprised. "Really?"

"No, of course not," said Ian. "It's a nightmare! What else could it be when you've got two people who keep asking if you're okay or want a cup of tea?"

"They're just being nice," said Amar.

"Well I don't want them to be nice," snapped Ian. "I want them to get on with their lives so I can just get on with mine!"

Amar fell silent at this outburst. He drank his Coke and crunched another ice cube while Ian stared into space.

"So I take it you still haven't heard from her?" said Amar.

Ian shook his head. "Not a word."

"Do you think that's a good or bad thing?"

"It's hard to say. On the one hand it means in theory we're still together. But on the other it could be that's she's simply plucking up the guts to tell me it's all over."

"I don't think it's all over, mate. Rukmani and I were talking about it last night and we agreed that you guys are too good together to split like this."

"And what did Rukmani have to say about my little stunt that got Emma sacked? Did she happen to mention what she would have done if she had been in Emma's shoes?"

Amar nodded. "She might have said the odd word about it. Something along the lines of if ever I did anything like that to her, she would set fire to everything I owned and then set fire to me too!"

"But would she forgive you?"

"What you've got to understand, mate, is that my Rukmani's quite a passionate woman. It's in her blood. Forgiveness doesn't come easily to her. Her dad still hates me for a joke I made about his moustache eleven years ago. But to answer your question, no. In fact her exact words were, 'Not in a million years.'"

Back at the office, Ian tried to throw himself into work in the hope of blocking out Amar's words but the harder he tried, the less he could do it. By three o'clock he had stopped even pretending to work and was simply staring out the window.

Mostly, Ian wanted to talk to Emma. To tell her how sorry he was and how he would do anything to get her back. A few times he even picked up the phone, but then he remembered how she had tearfully begged him not to make contact until she was ready to talk to him.

Thinking he would do a shop run for anyone in need of a can of drink or a bar of chocolate, Ian stood up and started taking orders from his fellow workmates. As not even management should be left out, Ian headed to Douglas's office, knocked on his door and walked in.

"Hi Doug," said Ian. "I was just wondering if . . ."

Ian didn't finish his sentence. He suddenly knew what he had to do. For a long moment the two men stood looking at each other blankly.

"Are you all right?" asked Douglas. "You look a bit funny."

"As it happens, Douglas, I'm not the slightest bit all right," said Ian. "And I haven't been all right since Emma left."

"Not again," said Douglas. "I thought we'd moved on from all that."

"You might have," said Ian, "but I haven't. The thing is, Douglas, you shouldn't have sacked her."

"Come on, Ian," replied Douglas. "You know as well as I do that I had no choice."

"But you sacked the wrong person."

"What are you saying? Has new evidence come to light?"

Ian shook his head. "I did it, Doug. It was me. I sent the email from Emma's computer. I wanted her to get sacked because I was sick of her messing things up for me at work."

There was a silence.

"You do know that I'll have to check out what you've said and, if it's true, I'll have no choice but to sack you?"

Ian nodded. "That's fine. It is all true. But it doesn't matter any more because I quit. Doug, I thought this job was the best thing in my life but it turns out that I was wrong. The best thing in my life is a beautiful, bright, funny girl called Emma Richards and the only thing in the world that matters to me is to get her to come back to me."

Chapter 18

Ian left the office unsure where to go next. He had to talk to Emma but first he had to find her. It was just after four. Would she be at home or might she already have found herself a new job and be out at work? Ian decided to try her mobile and hope that she would answer the call, but the phone rang out before directing him to her voicemail. Ian had to make a decision. To leave a message or not? He took a deep breath and started. "Emma, it's me. I know you asked me not to call you. I know you need time to sort out your head. It's just . . . it's just . . ." Ian struggled to finish his sentence. "It's just that . . . well . . . I need to speak to you. Things have changed and I need to speak to you right away. Okay, I'll leave it at that. I just want you to know, Em, I really do love you. I love you with my whole heart. And there isn't anything, and I do mean *anything at all*, that I wouldn't do if we could be together again."

Ian looked up at the grey sky. It looked like rain and he only had a few minutes before he got soaked to the skin, so he decided to make his way home and wait for Emma there. He pulled up his jacket collar and tried to walk as quickly as he could up the hill towards Five Ways. In fact he was so busy walking as quickly as he could that he failed to see someone walking just as fast in the opposite direction. Both he and the other person came to a sudden halt. Ian was about to apologise but he found he couldn't speak because standing there right in front of him was Emma.

"I just . . . I just . . . I just called you," said Ian. "How did you get here so quickly?"

Emma rolled her eyes. "I've got a time machine. You must have noticed it in the house? It's big and blue and shaped like an old-fashioned police box."

"So what are you saying? This was an accident?"

Emma nodded. "They do happen, you know."

"Yeah . . . but . . ." Ian's voice trailed off. If it wasn't an accident and Emma had been on her way to see him, then the last thing he wanted was to make a big deal about it in case she changed her mind.

"It's fine," said Emma. "You can relax, I'm not stalking you. I was only coming this way because I got a call from HR this morning to say that I could pick up my final pay cheque. I'm meeting up with Rukmani in an hour for coffee and then I'll be out of your way."

"But that's not what I want," said Ian.

Emma shrugged. "Well we can't always get what we want, can we?"

Ian looked into her eyes and saw that she was still hurting as much as when he had first told her about his betrayal. "I'm just really glad to see you," he said. He took in a full view of her. "You look well," he said. "Really well."

"That's what being unhappy does for you if you can't eat," she said. "And you're not the first to notice I've lost weight. Everyone I know keeps telling me that I look wonderful. I'm thinking I ought to get my heart broken by the person I trust most in the whole world a bit more often. You know, maybe every few months, like liposuction and Botox combined, only cheaper."

There was a long silence and then Ian spoke. "You do know that I'm sorry, don't you?" he said quietly. "I meant every word of my message just now. I would do anything for you, absolutely anything. All you have to do is say the word."

"Anything?"

"Yes, anything at all."

"So I could ask you to walk over broken glass and you'd do it?"

"In a second," said Ian.

"I could ask you to give away all those stupid comics of yours and you'd take them straight up to Oxfam?"

"I wouldn't even blink an eye," said Ian.

"Okay," said Emma. "How about this? How about if I asked you to turn around right now, go back to work, knock on Douglas's door and tell him the truth about what really happened with those emails? Would you do that?"

Ian shook his head.

"I knew it," said Emma. "You *do* love that job more than you love me."

"No, it's not that," said Ian, taking Emma's hand.

"What is it then?"

"I've already done it," said Ian. "I told Douglas everything this morning – about the email and why I did it. And I told him for one reason and one reason only, Em. Because without you, nothing else matters. I don't care about my job. I don't care about having a laugh. I don't care about any of it, if it means I can't have you."

There was a silence. Ian couldn't work out what Emma was thinking. Was she about to give him a second chance or was she going to kick him out of her life forever?

"What do you say, Em? What do you say to giving me a second chance?"

"I don't know," said Emma. "Part of me wants to forgive you because despite your many, many faults I love you more than life itself. But then part of me wants to give you a punch in the face."

"So do it."

"What?"

"Punch me in the face."

Emma looked horrified. "I'm not going to punch you in the face! What do you think I am?"

"It will make you feel better."

Emma shook her head. "I can tell you right now it won't make me feel better."

"It will," said Ian. "I promise you." He reached across to her and held up her hands. "Just make a fist, pull it back and let go."

"Ian Greening," said Emma, "I am not going to punch you in the face."

"Yeah, you will," said Ian. Emma's hands were still in the air and she had now made a fist with her right one. "All you need is a little bit of help."

"Like what?"

"I don't know," said Ian, "what would do

the trick? Me saying how much I hated it when you made me eat homemade sandwiches . . . or how I was annoyed that the Ad Girls stopped flirting with me? Or that I couldn't stand the book club you started or . . . or how much I loathed your cute cat calendar or . . ."

Ian hadn't finished when a small but well formed fist flew through the air at high speed and landed on his nose with such force that he span around twice before falling to the floor.

"I thought you said you weren't going to hit me!" cried Ian as blood poured from his nose.

"I know I did," said Emma. "But that was before you started having a go at my cute cat calendar." She knelt down, pulled a bunch of tissues from her bag, and held them to Ian's nose.

"You were right about one thing though," said Emma, as she helped Ian to his feet.

"What was that?"

"Punching you in the face really did make me feel a whole lot better." And without another word she wrapped her arms around Ian, and as the grey skies finally opened up and it began to rain, they shared a long kiss. And although Ian knew that they were not only both out of work but in danger of catching their death of cold, he was also aware that now they had each other again, everything would be okay in the end.

Quick Reads 📖

Books in the Quick Reads series

Quick Reads 📖

Great stories, great writers, great entertainment

Quick Reads are brilliantly written short new books by bestselling authors and celebrities. Whether you're an avid reader who wants a quick fix or haven't picked up a book since school, sit back, relax and let Quick Reads inspire you.

We would like to thank all our partners in the Quick Reads project for their help and support:

Arts Council England
The Department for Business, Innovation and Skills
NIACE
unionlearn
National Book Tokens
The Reading Agency
National Literacy Trust
Welsh Books Council
Basic Skills Cymru, Welsh Assembly Government
The Big Plus Scotland
DELNI
NALA

Quick Reads would also like to thank the Department for Business, Innovation and Skills; Arts Council England and World Book Day for their sponsorship and NIACE for their outreach work.

Quick Reads is a World Book Day initiative.
www.quickreads.org.uk   www.worldbookday.com

Other resources

Enjoy this book? Find out about all the others from **www.quickreads.org.uk**

Free courses are available for anyone who wants to develop their skills. You can attend the courses in your local area. If you'd like to find out more, phone 0800 66 0800.

For more information on developing your basic skills in Scotland, call The Big Plus free on 0808 100 1080 or visit www.thebigplus.com

Join the Reading Agency's Six Book Challenge at www.sixbookchallenge.org.uk

Publishers Barrington Stoke (www.barringtonstoke.co.uk) and New Island (www.newisland.ie) also provide books for new readers.

The BBC runs an adult basic skills campaign. See www.bbc.co.uk/raw.

www.worldbookday.com